I0748432

Acorn High School

Acorn High School

Acorn Dragons vs Shallow Falls Bears

Josh Zimmer

Superstar Speedsters

Copyright © 2020 by

All rights reserved. No part of this book may be reproduced in any manner whatsoever without written permission except in the case of brief quotations embodied in critical articles and reviews.

First Printing, 2020

Dedicated to the fantasy genre!

INSPIRATION

The book is inspired by werewolves, and other fantasy creatures!

CONTENTS

ACORN HIGH SCHOOL

Welcome to Fantasyville! In Fantasyville, there are two sections of the city! In one section, humans live in their houses, attend school, hang out with friends and family, and have fun. In the other section, zombies and other fantasy creatures live together, and hang out with each other. The government of Fantasyville doesn't like fantasy creatures hanging out with humans, but the city has changed their ways recently. The government has passed a law that fantasy creatures can attend school with the humans. In Fantasyville, high school students attend Acorn High School to expand their knowledge, and hang out with other students. Justin is a werewolf, and he lived in a blue house all by himself in Fantasyville. A couple of years ago, Justin's parents died in a fiery explosion, when a mad scientist experimented on them for the government. Justin lived a healthy life all by himself. Justin works out on a daily basis, and he is very athletic. Justin's dream was to join the high school football team. Justin laid in his room, under his bed sheets on the bed. The sun shined in Justin's window. Justin threw the bed sheets off of his head, and yawned! Justin climbed out of bed, and walked out of his room. Justin walked in to the bathroom, and locked the door. Justin turned on the shower, and took off his clothes. Justin walked in to the shower, and closed the shower door. Justin washed his hair, and cleaned his body. Justin washed his arms, and legs. Justin rehydrated his body! Justin turned off the shower, and opened the shower door. Justin dried himself with the towel! Justin put on his clothes, and brushed his hair. Justin brushed his teeth! Justin walked out of the bathroom. Justin walked in to the living room, and put his backpack on. Justin walked out the front door. Justin walked down the sidewalk. Justin walked on to the school bus. Justin walked to his seat on the bus. The humans on the school bus were terrified in fear, next to the window. Justin walked to the back of the school bus, and sat next to the window. Justin put his headphones in to his ears, as he listened to music on his phone. The school bus started up, and drove to Acorn High School. The school bus stopped at Acorn High School, and opened the bus doors. The students got up from their seats, and walked out of the bus doors. Justin got up from his seat, and took the head phones out of his ears. Justin put his phone in to his pocket. Justin walked out of the bus doors, and walked on to the sidewalk. Justin walked past the flag pole! Justin walked toward the doors for Acorn High School, and blended in to the crowd of students. Justin walked through the doors for Acorn High School. Justin walked through the hallway. The hallway was filled with students and teachers. The students were organizing their lockers, and hanging out with each other. The teachers were energizing themselves for the day, by reviewing their lesson plans and waking their brains up. Justin walked toward his locker. Justin stood at his locker, and turned the knob on the locker. Justin opened his locker, and organized it. Peter walked toward Justin, and pulled his tail. Justin yelped, and turned around. Peter said, "I am sorry that I have startled you, but I wanted to say hello!" Justin growled and said, "You could of tapped me on the shoulder. Pulling my tail was rude for a human." Peter said, "I am sorry, I am not used to interacting with a werewolf." Justin said, "It is fine, It is just a little reminder for next time." Peter smiled and said, "Cool, hope I see you around the area." Justin said, "Me too, you're a cool human to hang out with." Peter walked down the hallway toward his class. Justin continued organizing his locker. Justin closed his locker, and walked toward the water fountain. Justin drank out of the water fountain, and rehydrated himself. The bell rang in the background. The other students walked to their classes. The teachers walked out of the teachers lounge, and walked to their classrooms. Justin walked to his class. Justin stood in front of the door for his Algebra class. Justin turned the door knob, and walked in to the classroom. The other students stared at him. Justin walked to the back of the classroom, and sat at the empty desk. The algebra teacher's name was Matt. Matt was standing in front of the whiteboard. Matt wrote a Algebra equation on the whiteboard. Justin took his textbook out of his bag, and put it on his desk. Justin opened the textbook, and listened to Matt, while he was solving the equation on the whiteboard. The other students were writing notes in their notebooks, while Justin spun his pencil in his paws. The bell rang in the background. The other students put their supplies back in to their bags, and got up from their seats. Justin put his textbook and pencil in to his bag, and zipped it up. Justin got up from his seat, and put his bag on his back. Justin walked out of the classroom, and in to the hallway. Justin walked toward the water fountain. Justin drank out of the water fountain, and rehydrated himself. Flash walked toward Justin, and pushed him in to the locker. Justin laid against the locker, while Flash towered over him. Justin growled at Flash and said, "What is your problem?" Flash said, "Awww the little wolf wants to pick a fight with a human." Flash sped in to Justin, and smashed him in to the wall. Justin growled, and sharpened his claws. Justin punched Flash in the chest. Justin's claws ripped through Flash's shirt. Flash slid backwards! Justin sped in to Flash, and grabbed him by the neck. Justin stabbed his claws in to Flash's neck. Blood poured on the ground, as Justin lifted Flash in to the air. Justin threw Flash in to the wall! Flash laid on the ground, in a puddle of blood. Justin walked in to the men's bathroom. Harry, one of the other students helped Flash get up from the ground. Harry walked Flash to the nurse's office. Justin walked to the sink in the men's bathroom, and washed his fur. Justin walked out of the men's bathroom, and walked to the announcement board in the hallway. Justin read the announcement board! The announcement board said, "Football Tryouts are open! Come to the gym, if you're interested!" Justin said, "Football is the perfect sport to show the school that werewolves can be trusted." Justin walked toward the nurse's office. Justin walked in to the nurse's office. Ash, the nurse said, "Hey Justin, what's up! Is everything ok?"

Justin said, "I am here to check up on Flash!" Ash said, "Flash is fine, I cleaned the blood from his wounds, he is able to play football with the other team members." Flash was sitting on the chair, drinking a bottle of water. Justin said, "I was thinking of joining the football team." Ash said, "Cool, I heard that they opened tryouts in the gym." Justin said, "Yep, I was going to participate in the tryouts." Flash said, "Good luck in the tryouts, wolf! Football is a dangerous sport for a fluffball like you." Justin said, "I am willing to take the challenge, and prove you wrong." Flash said, "It would be entertaining to watch!" Justin walked out of the nurse's office. Justin walked down the hallway. Justin walked to the gym. Justin pushed the door open open, and walked in to the gym. Dodgeballs flew in the air, and hit Justin in the chest. Justin smashed in to the wall. Justin laid against the wall. The dodgeballs bounced on to the ground. Miles blew his whistle, and the other students walked to the side of the room, and put their bags on. The other students walked out of the gym. Justin walked to Miles. Justin said, "I am here to sign up for football tryouts." Miles said, "It isn't normal for a werewolf to tryout for the football team." Justin said, "Yeah, I want to shake things up for the football team." The football team walks in to the gym. James, the quarterback, walks up to Justin. James said, "I heard that you want to try out for the football team." Justin said, "Yep!" James said, "Prove your worth to the football team, fluffball." James waves the rest of the football team over. The rest of the football team walks to the middle of the gym, and get in to tackling position. Justin walks in to the passing position. James grabs a football, and passes it to Justin. Justin catches the football, and runs to the other side of the gym. The rest of the football players chase after Justin. Justin stiff arms one of the football players. The football player rolled on the ground. James was amazed by Justin's performance. The football player got up from the ground. The other football players got out of position, and stood next to James. Justin walked to James. James said, "Good work Justin, you look like a good fit for our team. James and Justin shook hands, as the gym teacher smiled in the background. The bell rang in the background. James said, "the football game is later today, lets get you suited up in your football uniform." Justin nodded, as the football players walked to the locker room. James walked to the locker room with the other football players. Justin followed James and the rest of the football team to the locker room. Justin and the football team walked in to the locker room. Justin was amazed at how big the locker room was. James walked to the closet, where the football uniforms hung. James gave a football uniform to Justin. Justin sat on the bench, and put the football uniform on. James said, "The football uniform looks great on you." Justin nodded, as he high fived James. James high fived Justin. James said, "Let's practice your tackling abilities. James got in to position! Justin sped toward James and tackled him in to the ground. Justin got up from the ground. James got up from the ground. James said, "That was perfect!" The coach for the football team walked in to the locker room, and blew his whistle. Coach Andrew said, "It's time for the football game, lets put on our football uniforms, and walk on to the field." The football team put their uniforms on. The football team got up from the bench. Coach Andrew and the football team walked to the football field. Coach Andrew and the football team walked on to the football field. Shallow Falls Bears were on the football field, waiting for Coach Andrew and the football team. Shallow Falls Bears represent Shallow Falls High School, that is located down the road from Acorn High School. Coach Andrew's football team were the Acorn Dragons. The Acorn Dragons and the Shallow Falls Bears were growling at each other, while the referee stood next to them. Peter, the quarterback for the Shallow Falls Bears, and Justin were growling at each other. Peter said, "Awwww, the football team is trying to be tough. They recruited a little wolf to help them." Justin growled and said, "Who are you calling, little wolf?" Justin walked toward Peter and pushed him in to the water cooler. Peter slid backwards, as the water cooler shook. Peter said, "You want me to beat you up, fluff. I can knock some sense in to you." Peter tackled Justin in to the football field. Justin laid on the football field, as Peter punched Justin's football helmet. Justin growled, and bit Peter's arm with his fangs. The rest of the football team growled, and pounced on Justin, to hold him down. The rest of the Acorn Dragons team helped Justin, by throwing Shallow Falls Bears players off of him. Justin growled, and stabbed his claws in to the Shallow Falls Bears players. Justin threw the players off of him. The football players for the Shallow Falls Bears rolled on the football field. Justin got up from the ground, and picked up Peter by his gloved paw. Justin smashed Peter through the table. Peter laid on the ground, as the water cooler fell and poured water on top of him. Peter got up from the ground, and grabbed Justin by the neck. Peter threw Justin at the bench on the sideline for the Acorn Dragons. Justin smashed through the cooler, and the cooler poured water on top of Justin's uniform. Peter held Justin on the ground, and pulled his helmet off. Peter threw Justin's helmet on to the ground. Justin growled, and sharpened his claws. Justin scratched Peter's arm with his claws. Peter slid backwards! Justin got up from the ground. The referee blew his whistle, and directed Justin and Peter back to their sideline. Justin and Peter stood next to their teams. Coach Andrew said, "Save your strength for the football field." The football team nodded, as they sat on the sideline bench. The football team for the Shallow Falls Bears sat on their sideline bench. The referee blew his whistle, and put the football on the field. The Acorn Dragons football team and the Shallow Falls football team walked on to the football field, and got in to their positions. James and the Acorn Dragons offense hiked the ball, while the Shallow Falls defense growled at them. James stepped backwards and threw the football to Justin. The Shallow Falls defense ran after Justin. Justin stiff armed the defense player on to the field as he ran for the first down. Justin dived on to the football field for the first down. The Acorn Dragons got further down the football field in to the red zone. James hiked the football, and threw it to Justin. Justin caught the football, and scored the touchdown. The students cheered in the bleachers, and the mascot backflipped in the air on the football field. The offense for the Acorn Dragons and the defense for the Shallow Falls Bears walked to their sidelines, and sat on the bench. Peter and the offense for the Shallow Falls

Bears walked on to the football field. The defense for the Acorn Dragons walked on to the football field. The offense and the defense got in to their positions. Peter hiked the ball, and analyzed the football field. The defense ran after Peter. The defense player was about to tackle Peter in to the field, but Peter side stepped out of the way. Peter kicked the defense player in the chest with his leg. The defense player rolled on the football field. Peter threw the football player to Miles. Miles ran down the football field, and scored the touchdown. The defense player got up from the football field, and walked to the sideline. The defense player was disappointed in himself, as the offense and the defense walked off the field. The football game continued for 3 more quarters on the football field. The football game was tied 21 - 21 on the scoreboard, with 2 minutes left on the clock. The offense for the Acorn Dragons were on the field, and the defense for the Shallow Falls Bears were growling at them. James hiked the ball, and he got in to position. The offense players ran their routes on the field. The defense players growled, and ran after James. Matt ran to James, and tackled him in to the football field for a sack. The referee blew the whistle, and stopped the clock. James got up from the football field. There was 1 minute left on the clock! The offense and the defense got in to their positions on the football field. James hiked the ball, and the offense players ran their routes. The defense players growled at the offense players. James threw the football to Justin. Justin caught the ball, and ran down the football field. The clock was ticking down, as Justin ran toward the red zone. The defense players ran after Justin. Justin stiff armed the defense players. The defense players rolled on to the football field. Justin scored the touchdown, and the clock ran out. The Acorn Dragons won the football game. Peter, and the rest of the Shallow Falls Bears walked on to the football field. James and the rest of the Acorn Dragons walked toward the Shallow Falls bears and shook their hands. James said, "That was a good game!" Peter said, "I agree, thanks for the fun." The Acorn Dragons and the Shallow Falls Bears walked off of the football field. The Acorn Dragons walked in to the locker room, and sat on the bench. The football players took off their helmets. The Acorn Dragons wiped the sweat from their bodies with their towels. The football players for the Acorn Dragons walked in to the shower area, and took off their football uniforms. They put their football uniforms in to the basket, and took the rest of their clothes off. The football players took a shower and washed the dirt off of their bodies. Justin took off his football uniform, and threw it in to the basket. Justin took the rest of his clothes off, and took a shower. Justin washed the dirt off of his body. Justin and the rest of the football players walked out of the shower, and put their clothes back on. Justin, and the rest of the football team walked out of the locker room, and sat on the football field. The sun was setting, and the moon shined bright on the football field. James and Justin sat next to each other, and watched the stars in the sky. It got cold outside, so the football team walked back in to the locker room. The football team hugged each other, as they went to their assigned beds in the sleeping section of the locker room. Justin sat on his bed, and went under the bed sheets. Justin fell asleep, and closed his eyes. The sun rose over Acorn High School. The football team woke up from their beds, and stretched their legs. The football team walked out of the locker room. The football team walked in to the gym! The football team walked in to the hallway. The students of Acorn High School cheered them on for support. Justin shook hands with the other students, as he smiled at them. The students supported the football team's success on the football field. Justin was glad, that he was part of the football team. Justin walked toward his locker, and opened it. Justin reorganized his locker! Justin hydrated himself at the water fountain. Flash walked up to Justin, and tapped him on the shoulder. Justin said, "Hey, Flash, what's up?" Flash said, "I would like to congratulate you on winning the football game with the rest of the football team." Justin said, "Thanks Flash, you're the best!" Flash said, "No problem, fluff ball. Thanks to your help, the school and the city supports werewolves and humans hanging out together." Justin and Flash high fived each other. Flash walked to his locker. Justin walked down the hallway. Justin walked out of the school, and sat on the steps. James walked out of the school, and sat next to Justin. James wrapped his arm around Justin. James said, "I am glad that you joined the football team." Justin said, "Me too, we are a good team!" James and Justin smiled at each other. The sun was shining on the school, while they sat on the steps.

Josh Zimmer is an crazy individual with an extreme imagination. He loves to have fun by listening to music, writing stories, and playing video games of various genres such as platforming, multiplayer online games, role playing games, and sports games. His favorite technology brands are Nintendo and Microsoft. They are wonderful role models for the industry. He commands an army of cats to his will with hugs, love, and snacks. He makes the cats purr and meow with happiness.

www.ingramcontent.com/pod-product-compliance
Lightning Source LLC
Chambersburg PA
CBHW070619310726
48982CB00001B/123

* 9 7 8 0 5 7 8 7 5 9 4 0 1 *